Wish

Wishing Traditions
Around the World

by Roseanne Thong

art by Elisa Kleven

chronicle books · san francisco

How in the world do you make a wish?

Come follow and you'll see
the many ways to make a wish
wherever home may be!

Racing swiftly through the graves
we launch our giant kites,
so they will carry wishes
as they soar to heaven's heights.

In Guatemala, children fly giant kites in cemeteries on November 1 (All Saints' Day) and November 2 (All Souls' Day), to honor the dead and carry wishes up to the gods. These colossal, circular kites can be the size of small cars (15 feet), while giant display kites on the ground can reach 100 feet in diameter! They are made from strips of paper attached to a bamboo frame. Their colors are dazzling and their patterns look like bright tapestries.

We tie our wishes to bamboo
the seventh of July,
as children look for stars that tell
a story in the sky.

In Japan, children make wishes at the Star Festival, or Tanabata (*tan-AH-BAH-TAH*), each year on July 7. They write their desires on narrow strips of colored paper and tie them to bamboo branches. This festival originates in a legend about a shepherd and a fairy weaver who fall in love—but can see each other only one night of the year—the seventh of the month. On this night, children look for two bright stars in the summer sky—Altair and Vega—that represent the shepherd and weaver.

Upon a Persian carpet
we prepare a New Year's treat
with pudding, nuts, and jujubes
to keep our wishes sweet.

Before Noruz (*now-ROOZ*), or Iranian New Year, families spread a special "cloth of seven dishes" on a Persian carpet, the traditional place to eat, or on the dinner table. Seven symbolic foods are placed upon it, each one representing one of the seven wishes: love, health, happiness, prosperity, joy, patience, and beauty.

We take a copper penny
and we place it in our shoe.
The left one is the best, of course,
though either one will do.

In Russia (as in other countries), if you find a lucky coin and place it in your left shoe, you will have a wish come true and good luck on your road ahead. Russians also make wishes by throwing coins over their shoulder at Moscow's Red Square in front of the Resurrection Gate, the place from which all distances in Russia are measured.

A lonely weasel dashing by
means luck's in store for you.
He'll hold your wish until the day
it's ready to come true.

The Zulus of South Africa know and love a small, fast-footed animal called the striped weasel. These playful creatures live and hunt in groups and are rarely seen alone. They race about the countryside, nose-to-tail, like interlinked cars on a train. If you see one by itself, make a wish quickly! It is said the weasel will carry your wish for as long as it takes to come true.

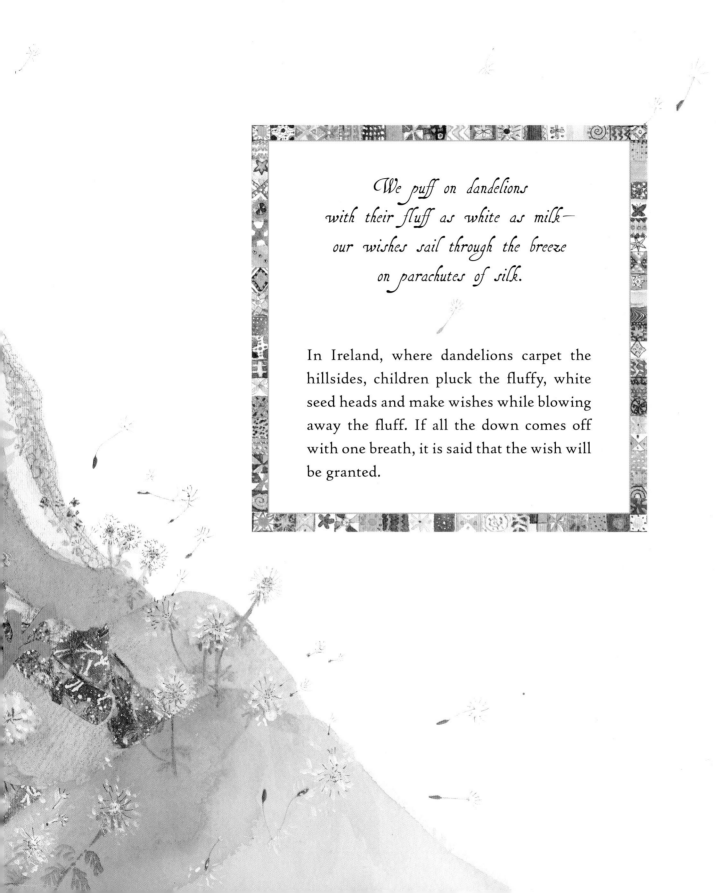

We puff on dandelions
with their fluff as white as milk—
our wishes sail through the breeze
on parachutes of silk.

In Ireland, where dandelions carpet the
hillsides, children pluck the fluffy, white
seed heads and make wishes while blowing
away the fluff. If all the down comes off
with one breath, it is said that the wish will
be granted.

A peacock feather shimmering
with purple, green, and blue,
slipped in between a notebook page,
will help our dreams come true.

In India, school children make secret wishes on lucky peacock feathers, and keep them safe between the pages of their school notebooks, journals, or diaries. Though the wishes are often about success at school, they can be about any hope or desire.

We offer lovely flowers
to the goddess of the deep.
While jumping seven waves,
we toss in combs for her to keep.

In Brazil, people go to the beach on New Year's Day, jump seven waves, and throw offerings of flowers and hair combs into the sea while making a wish. They believe that Yemanja (*yay-mahn-JHAH*), the goddess of the sea, will accept these offerings and make their wishes come true.

*We toss our coins and make a wish
whenever we're in Rome.
Three for marriage, two for love,
and one to come back home!*

In Italy, people toss coins into Rome's famous Trevi Fountain and make wishes. An old legend says that if you throw three coins over your left shoulder, you'll get married. If you throw two coins, you'll fall in love, and if you throw one, you'll return to Rome.

We roll our wishes into scrolls,
tied to an orange, tight,
then aiming for a banyan branch,
we throw with all our might!

In China, people write their wishes down on sheets of lucky red and gold paper covered with blessings and words of good fortune. These are rolled into scrolls, fastened with string to a mandarin orange for weight, and tossed into a wishing tree. It is said your wish will come true if the scroll and the orange catch on a branch.

Stirring Christmas pudding
on a sunny, summer day
is how our family members
make warm wishes come their way.

Australians love eating plum pudding for Christmas, a tradition originally from England. This pudding is similar to American fruitcakes—dark brown steamed dough filled with dried fruits and nuts, with flaming brandy poured over it. The whole family gathers to make the pudding, stirring it three times from east to west while making a wish. Because Australia is in the southern hemisphere, December falls in the summer.

Plum Pudding
1 c. flour
1 lb. raisins
1 lb. currants
1 c. almonds
1 T cinnamon
1 T mace
1 c. sugar
7 egg yolks

In Jerusalem's old quarter,
family members big and small
place wishes into ancient cracks
along the Western Wall.

In Israel, Jewish people from all over the world come to pray and make wishes at Jerusalem's Western Wall by slipping a piece of paper (called a *kvitlach*) into the cracks. The Western Wall is all that remains of the second Temple of Solomon, which was built about fifteen hundred years ago.

We blow an eyelash off our fist
and make a secret wish,
perhaps for a piñata
or our favorite party dish.

Many cultures share the belief that if an eyelash accidentally falls off, you can make a wish by blowing it away. Children in Mexico put it on the back of their fist, close their eyes tight, and make a wish as they blow three times. The number three is believed to be magic in many cultures, as in the old saying "the third time's a charm."

Our brightly glowing lotus boats
sail off beneath the moon.
They tow away bad luck so that
our wishes come true soon.

In Thailand, children make wishes each November during Loi Krathong (*loy-KRAH-tong*) Festival. People of all ages build or purchase *krathongs*—little boats made from banana leaves or paper, and folded to look like lotus flowers. These boats are filled with candles, coins, flowers, and incense and set afloat at a river's edge. They are said to carry away bad luck so that good wishes can come true.

We light the candles on the cake
before our birthday games.
Then close our eyes and wish real hard—
And puff!—blow out the flames!

American children make silent wishes while blowing out the candles on their birthday cake. This is done after family and friends sing "Happy Birthday to You," a song popularized in 1931. It is said that blowing out all the candles in one breath will make the wish come true, but only if it's kept secret.

Children all around the world
hope wishes will come true.

This is the way we make a wish...
now tell us what you do!

SHALOM
שָׁלוֹם
PEACE

Australia

Long ago, a ring, a coin, a thimble, and a button were baked into the plum pudding. Finding the ring in your slice meant you'd marry soon; the coin meant you would have wealth; and the thimble (for women) or button (for men) meant you would remain single. Traditionally, plum pudding was made a year in advance and served the following Christmas.

Brazil

Many Brazilians are descendants of Africans brought over as slaves, so many Brazilian traditions have African roots. Yemanja is closely related to the west-African goddess Yemaya. Yemanja loves and protects children and is known as "everyone's mother." People honor her by wearing white and offering gifts of flowers, perfume, and combs.

China

In China, banyan trees are said to grant wishes, probably because of their large roots that twist and curve into amazing shapes. It is easy to imagine these roots having special powers. Long ago, people attached potatoes, carrots, or even rocks to their wishing scrolls to give them weight. Eventually, oranges replaced everything else, because they represent gold and riches.

Guatemala

Guatemala's 3,000-year-old kite flying festival is a mixture of different beliefs. In ancient times, Guatemalans worshiped many gods. When the Spanish conquistadors arrived, they brought the Catholic religion to Guatemala. These beliefs mixed over time, and today the giant kites carry wishes up to many gods and saints, and beloved ancestors.

India

The peacock is India's national bird and considered lucky. It said that Lord Muruga, one of the Indian gods, rides on the back of a peacock. Even grown-ups save peacock feathers when they find them, as a way to show respect for the gods.

Iran

The number seven has been considered sacred in Iran since ancient times. The seven dishes include lentil or wheat sprouts, apples, pudding, vinegar, garlic, sumac berries, and jujubes (a type of small, red date). Other lucky symbols placed on the cloth might include a bowl of goldfish, mirrors, candles, coins, and hard-boiled eggs.

Ireland

For hundreds of years, dandelions were used as a folk remedy to cure different kinds of illness. This may have led people to believe they were magical. Today, people eat all parts of the plant. The leaves are cooked as vegetables, the flowers are used for dandelion jelly and wine, and the roots are boiled to make a tea or coffee substitute.

Israel

The Western Wall is also known as the Wailing Wall, because people used to cry there and remember the destruction of King Solomon's first temple, built on the same spot. Jewish people consider it the most sacred spot in Jerusalem, and pray there day and night.

Italy

In ancient times, sailors threw coins into the waves to ask sea gods for a safe voyage. That custom later developed into the tradition of tossing coins into fountains and wells to have wishes granted. At Trevi Fountain, people throw coins before a statue of Neptune—god of the sea—following this same tradition.

Japan

In addition to making wishes, Japanese children place colorful streamers outside their homes on Tanabata. These streamers represent the fairy weaver's threads, as well as luck for fishing and farming.

Mexico

There are different ways to wish on an eyelash. Some people place it on their left fist and press the palm of their right hand against it. If it sticks to their right hand, it is said that the wish will come true.

Russia

Coins are a symbol of wishes and good luck all over the world—especially luck with money. In some countries, people hide pennies when selling their house to ensure the new owners will have good luck. Brides often place a penny in their wedding shoe for luck, wealth, and good wishes.

South Africa

Zulu children grow up hearing folk stories about animals from the time they are very young: weasels, mongooses, rhinos, and elephants, among others. In one Zulu folktale, a weasel tricks the mighty lion. The Zulus' love for the weasel and other animals is very strong.

Thailand

The Loi Kathrong festival takes place on a full-moon night when the rainy season is over. It is a way to thank Mae Khongka, goddess of waters, for plentiful rainfall, and to apologize for polluting her waters during the year.

United States

The ancient Greeks are thought to have been the first to celebrate birthdays with round moon-shaped cakes to honor Artemis, the moon goddess. Later, they added candles to give the cakes a moonlike glow. Like many American customs, the traditions of birthday candles and birthday wishes are gifts from far away.

Look closely, and you'll find in this book 15 lucky symbols hiding in the pictures:

dolphin

elephant with trunk raised

frog

bell

key

goldfish in a bowl

rabbit

red snapper

stork

rainbow

turtle with a coin in its mouth

fish

dove

horseshoe

ladybug

Ireland

Italy

Israel

Iran

Russia

China

Japan

India

Thailand

South
Africa

Australia